FLY GUY
VS. THE
FLYSWATTER!

Tedd Arnold

CARTWHEEL BOOKS
An Imprint of Scholastic Inc.

For Brianna!

Library of Congress Cataloging-in-Publication Data
Arnold, Tedd.
Fly Guy vs. the fly swatter / Tedd Arnold. – 1st ed. p. cm.
Summary: Fly Guy unintentionally joins Buzz at school, and then goes
with his class on a field trip to a fly swatter factory.
ISBN 978-0-545-31286-8
[1. Flies–Fiction. 2. School field trips–Fiction.] I. Title. II.
Title: Fly Guy versus the fly swatter.
PZ7.A7379Fmv 2011
[E]– dc22
2010031381

ISBN 978-0-545-84870-1
10 9 8 7 6 5 4 3 2   17 18 19
Printed in the U.S.A.   40
This edition first printing, January 2015

A boy had a pet fly.
He named him Fly Guy.
And Fly Guy could
say the boy's name—

BUZZ!

Chapter 1

One day, Fly Guy was eating breakfast in Buzz's backpack.

Buzz grabbed his backpack
and went to school.

At school, Fly Guy
flew out.

Then the teacher said,
"We are going on a field trip
to tour a factory."

Buzz said, "Fly Guy, you can ride in my pocket."

The class rode the bus to the factory.

They arrived at the factory.

Chapter 2

A tour guide led the class inside.

Buzz said, "Fly Guy, stay down in my pocket!"

The tour guide said,
"Here is our flyswatter
museum."

"Here is where we make the flyswatters," she said. "You may each have one."

"Now," said the guide, "here is
Fred the Fly to tell you more!"

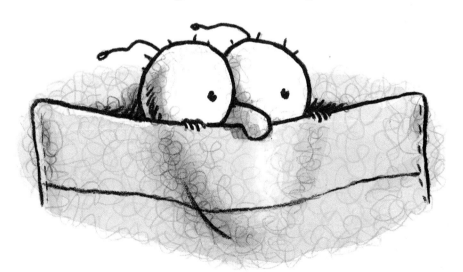

Fly Guy peeked out.

"Boys and girls," said Fred.
"We know flies play in slime."
Fly Guy nodded.

"Flies eat garbage!"
Fly Guy smiled.

"Flies are nasty!"

Fly Guy got mad.

"That's why, boys and girls,"
Fred the Fly shouted,
"we need . . .

the flyswatter of the future—
the **Super Swatter 6000!**"

Chapter 3

"Now let's see what the Super Swatter can do!" said Fred. "Bring out the fly!"

The tour guide brought
out a tiny fly in a jar.

"Release the fly!"
yelled Fred.

The Super Swatter
started swatting.

WHAP
WHAP
WHAP
WHAP
WHAP

Fly Guy cried,

Fly Guy flew to the little fly.

The Super Swatter kept swatting

Fly Guy took the fly
to an open window.

The Super Swatter kept swatting.

Fly Guy flew past
Fred the Fly.

WHAP

WHAP

WHAP

WHAP

WHAP

WHAP

WHAP

WHAP

The Super Swatter kept swatting.

Fly Guy flew past the
flyswatter machines.
The Super Swatter kept swatting

"Stop! Stop!" yelled Fred.
"Everyone out! No more
factory tours, ever!"

Back at school, the class made an art project. Everyone agreed—